I HERO

MONSTER HUNTER
ALIEN

STEVE BARLOW AND STEVE SKIDMORE
ILLUSTRATED BY PAUL DAVIDSON

EDGE

FRANKLIN WATTS

LONDON·SYDNEY

Franklin Watts
First published in Great Britain in 2018
by The Watts Publishing Group

Text © Steve Barlow and Steve Skidmore 2018
Illustrations © The Watts Publishing Group 2018
Cover design: Peter Scoulding
Executive Editor: Adrian Cole

ISBN 978 1 4451 5878 5
ebook ISBN 978 1 4451 5876 1
Library ebook ISBN 978 1 4451 5877 8

1 3 5 7 9 10 8 6 4 2

Printed and bound by CPI Group (UK) Ltd, Croydon, CR0 4YY

MIX
Paper from
responsible sources
FSC® C104740
www.fsc.org

Franklin Watts
An imprint of
Hachette Children's Group
Part of The Watts Publishing Group
Carmelite House
50 Victoria Embankment
London EC4Y 0DZ

An Hachette UK Company
www.hachette.co.uk

www.franklinwatts.co.uk

Mission Statement

You are the hero of this mission.

Each section of this book is numbered. At the end of most sections, you will have to make a choice. The choice you make will take you to a different section of the book.

Some of your choices will help you to complete the adventure successfully. But if you make the wrong choice, death may be the best you can hope for! Because even dying is better than being UNDEAD and becoming a slave of the monsters you have sworn to destroy!

Dare you go up against a world of monsters?

All right, then.

Let's see what you've got...

Introduction

You are an agent of **G.H.O.S.T.** — Global Headquarters Opposing Supernatural Threats.

Our world is under constant attack from supernatural horrors that lurk in the shadows. It's your job to make sure they stay there.

You have studied all kinds of monsters, and know their habits and behaviour. You are an expert in disguise, able to move among monsters in human form as a spy. You are expert in all forms of martial arts. G.H.O.S.T. has supplied you with weapons, equipment and other assets that make you capable of destroying any supernatural creature.

G.H.O.S.T.

You are based at Arcane Hall, a spooky and secret-laden mansion. Your butler, Cranberry, is another G.H.O.S.T. agent who assists you in all your adventures, providing you with information and backup.

Your life at Arcane Hall is comfortable and peaceful; but you know that at any moment, the G.H.O.S.T. High Command can order you into action in any part of the world...

Go to 1.

1

You are crouching in a dark cellar, hunting down a monster. You don't know what type of monster it is, but you have to deal with it before it deals with you!

You look at your MAAD — Monster And Alien Detector — on your wrist. It starts to flash red. There is an alien in the vicinity.

Your finger tightens on the trigger of your BAM gun. BAM stands for "Blasts All Monsters" — when the detector reveals the monster, you will be able to blast it!

You gasp in horror as the monster comes into view but there's a BIG problem — there's not just one monster, there are two!

To use your MAAD again, go to 8.
To use your BAM, go to 32.

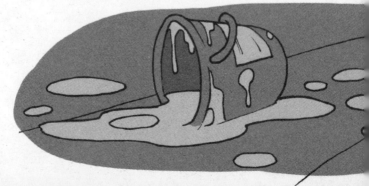

2

You set the BAM to single shot setting and fire at the first ALF. The alien disintegrates in a puff of smoke.

You aim again and a second ALF is vaporised.

However, the remaining ALFs turn their alien weapons on you. A volley of shock grenades and plasma bolts comes your way!

You see a flash of light as a fireball engulfs you and then there is nothing but blackness...

Sometimes a full-on attack is the only way to go! Go back to 1.

3

"That's what they've signed up for," you tell the general. "I'll take half a dozen."

You and the soldiers step through the portal and into the wormhole. It feels as though your body is being ripped apart as you travel through time and space.

Then there is a flash of light and you and the troops pass through the alien portal and into a huge metal chamber.

"I'll use the MAAD to check out if there are

any ALFs about," you tell the troops. You switch it on and it immediately flashes red. "That's strange," you say. "I can't see any ALFs... Detect!" you order the MAAD.

A laser beam shoots out and lights up on the troops one by one!

"Death to humans! Death to humans," chant the soldiers.

The troops are contaminated!

Before you can react, one of the troops hits you with his gun and you pass out.

Go to 44.

"Okay, the debrief can wait. Let's see what
G.H.O.S.T. has for us."

Cranberry switches on the comms screen to
reveal a stream of images and text.

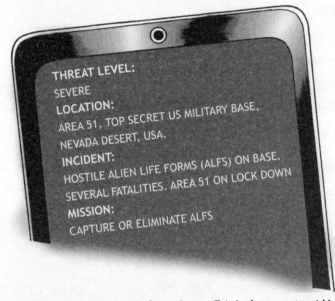

THREAT LEVEL:
SEVERE
LOCATION:
AREA 51, TOP SECRET US MILITARY BASE,
NEVADA DESERT, USA.
INCIDENT:
HOSTILE ALIEN LIFE FORMS (ALFS) ON BASE.
SEVERAL FATALITIES. AREA 51 ON LOCK DOWN
MISSION:
CAPTURE OR ELIMINATE ALFS

"So, the rumour that Area 51 is home to Alien
Life Forms is true," you say.

Cranberry nods. "G.H.O.S.T. have been
working with the US government for many years,
researching alien technology. How do you think
we gained the knowledge for all the weapons
that you use? Most of the ALFs at Area 51 have

been happy to work with us, so this incident is extremely puzzling."

"It looks like some of them wanted out," you say.

"Yes, but why?" he replies

"That's what I've got to find out. And then deal with them!"

To head to Area 51 on your own, go to 42.
To take Cranberry with you, go to 19.

5

Sometime later the prisoners are with you in the portal chamber. A troop of enemy ALFs stand with their weapons pointing at you, but they dare not attack in case you set off the bomb.

"Thanks for the delivery," you say. "Now, everybody out of the room, and we'll just head back over to Earth."

The ALF captain laughs. "Our master is already on Earth. It is only a matter of time before you are all under our control."

You wonder who or what the ALF is referring to.

The enemy aliens leave. You shut the door and blast the controls to make sure it stays shut.

You send the friendly ALFs through the wormhole and then place the gamma ray bomb at the mouth of the wormhole.

How long should I set the delay for? you wonder.

To set the bomb's delay timer to thirty minutes, go to 20.

To set it to two minutes, go to 31.

6

"Activate all defences!" you order.

"Defence systems activated," confirms the computer.

The incoming missile ALF hits the jet's defence shield and blows up.

You contact Cranberry to tell him about the missile-riding ALF!

"Strange," he says. "You'll need to be very careful."

"Thanks for stating the obvious." You guide the jet towards Area 51's landing strip.

Go to 45.

On reaching the command centre, you are introduced to General Walker.

"I didn't want G.H.O.S.T. involved in this," he says. "We can deal with it ourselves."

"It doesn't look like it," says a voice from across the room. You turn and see a woman dressed in military uniform. She holds out a hand. "Dr Dekka. I'm the director of Project Wormhole in Area 51."

To find out more about Project Wormhole, go to 46.

To find out more about the ALF situation on the base, go to 30.

8

You point your MAAD at the monsters.

"Detect!" you order. A red laser beam shoots out of the MAAD, targeting the monster on the left.

In an instant you blast at the creature. Your aim is spot on! The monster explodes, sending putrid lime green slime and guts splattering all around you. At the same time, the monster on the right vanishes before your eyes.

Go to 15.

9

You set your ZAP (Zero Alien Presence) and BAM weapons to max power. As the ALFs come into view, you blast them, taking out the majority of the enemy. However, the surviving ALFs fight back. They bombard you with lasers and mini missiles that explode around you. You realise that you are in a serious battle!

To find shelter, go to 48.
To continue the fight, go to 23.

"Take me to General Walker."

The captain points at a black SUV and you climb in. He sits in the driver's seat and sets off.

"Any ideas about why the ALFs attacked?" you ask him.

"I know exactly why," he replies. He suddenly slams his foot down on the accelerator, pulls the SUV into a tight turn and heads for a huge fuel tank!

"What are you doing?" you cry out.

"My masters will win. Death to humans, death to humans..."

You realise that the captain has somehow been taken over by the aliens!

To get out of the SUV, go to 40.
To attack the captain, go to 37.

11

You pull out your gun and point it at General Walker. "It all adds up to you being the wolf in sheep's clothing."

"You're making a big mistake," says the general.

"He's right," says Dr Dekka.

"What makes you say that?" you ask.

"Because I'm the master!"

You turn to see Dr Dekka transforming into an ALF. Before you can react, her tongue shoots out from her slavering jaws and into your mouth. You feel your mind slowly slipping away...

So near but so far! Go back to 1.

12

"Our ALFs set up a wormhole portal here on the base, connected to their homeworld," Dr Dekka explains.

"And I'm guessing unfriendly ALFs came through it?"

"Correct," says Dr Dekka. "They took back all our ALFs through the wormhole, claiming they were traitors. They also threatened to destroy Earth."

"That's what hostile aliens do," you say.

"But you've neutralised them. We should be okay," the doctor points out.

"As you said, there could be contamination of people on the base," you reply. "And what's to stop the enemy ALFs coming back through the wormhole? We should close it."

"We can close the wormhole this end," says Dr Dekka more urgently, "but the ALFs have locked a location onto this planet. They could open up another wormhole through their portal and invade anywhere on Earth."

The general interrupts. "The portal has taken us years to develop, and we need it to stay open to get those friendly ALFs back here."

To ask for Cranberry's advice, go to 24.

To close the wormhole on Earth, go to 21.

13

"Target missile and fire," you order the weapons system. It responds immediately.

A Poltergeist Sting Missile launches and streaks quickly through the sky. However, the alien simply spins the missile away, avoiding the Poltergeist. It continues its deadly course towards you.

"INCOMING MISSILE! INCOMING MISSILE!"

"Evasive action!" you order, but it is too late. There is a flash of light and an explosion and then silence...

Go back to 1.

14

You take out your BAM and point it at the ALF.

As you do so, he smiles. "Goodbye, Earthling," he growls and presses a button on a grenade. You are caught in the deadly explosion.

Blast! You made the wrong choice.
Go back to 1.

15

The cellar lights flash on. You shield your eyes against the sudden glare as a voice booms out from loudspeakers. It is Cranberry, your butler and fellow G.H.O.S.T. agent.

"Well done, Agent. You used the MAAD to reveal that the second monster was merely a virtual reality reflection of the first. That was a successful training session."

"Thanks, Cranberry." You wipe the slime from your eyes. "How do you make this stuff?"

"My special top secret recipe. It's been passed down the ages from Cranberry to Cranberry. Now, it's time for a debrief..."

Go to 25.

16

"I agree with the general," you reply. "It will be better for me to go on my own..."

Dr Dekka looks worried. "On your head be it," she says.

You take out your BAM and head to the wormhole's entrance.

"Good luck, Agent," says Dr Dekka.

You step carefully through the portal into the wormhole. It feels as though your body is being ripped apart as you travel through time and space.

Suddenly there is a flash of light and you pass through the alien portal and into a huge metal chamber.

"Surrender, Earthling!"

You look in horror and see several ALFs pointing some very serious weaponry at you. They were expecting you!

To fight the ALFs, go to 26.
To detonate the gamma ray bomb, go to 29.

17

"Are you okay, Captain?" you ask, reaching into your pack.

"Yes, why wouldn't I be?" replies the captain in a strange voice.

You point the MAAD device at him. "Detect!" A laser beam hits the captain. He's an ALF!

The captain leaps at you. He holds you in a vice-like grip.

"Death to humans!" he chants. The other troops raise their guns.

To order the troops to open fire, go to 34.
To fight the captain yourself, go to 43.

18

You decide that you will try and rescue the captured ALFs and move out of the chamber.

As you do so, you hear voices ahead of you and the squelching sounds of alien feet heading your way!

To fight the ALFs, go to 9.
To try and find a hiding place, go to 48.

19

"I'll need you to fly over with me," you say to Cranberry.

He shakes his head. "I need full access to G.H.O.S.T. data. If Area 51 is on lockdown, that will be difficult. I should stay here to co-ordinate the operation."

You realise that Cranberry is right. "OK, but keep me informed if you get any more info."

Go to 42.

20

You set the timer and step through the portal. Once again you feel as though you are being ripped apart. There is another flash of light, and you find yourself back in Area 51.

Dr Dekka, General Walker and the rescued ALFs are all waiting for you.

"Well done, Agent," says the general. "Did you set the timer?"

"Yes," you reply. "For thirty minutes."

"That's too long," replies Dr Dekka.

You scowl. "Did Cranberry come up with the right time?"

Dr Dekka smiles. "No... I did. Thirty minutes gave my people long enough to disarm the bomb, and follow you through the wormhole!"

Suddenly the room is full of explosions as dozens of enemy ALFs pour through the portal, weapons blazing. The general falls to the ground, dead.

The ALFs bow to Dr Dekka. "Master, your plan has worked."

"So you're the—" But your words are cut off as Dr Dekka transforms into an ALF and her tongue shoots out from her slavering jaws and into your mouth. You feel your mind slowly slipping away...

Welcome to the alien race! Go back to 1.

21

"I'm afraid those ALFs are lost to us," you say.
"We need to close the wormhole this end.
Take me to it."

Despite their protests, the doctor and
general lead you through steel-lined corridors
to the huge vault containing the entrance to
the wormhole.

"We need to shut this thing down," you say.

"I can't allow that!" cries the general. He
grabs hold of you. You slip through his grip but
stumble backwards and fall into the entrance
of the wormhole.

It feels as though your body is being ripped
apart as you travel through time and space.
You pass out.

Go to 44.

22

"The priority is to stop them getting to the
weapons centre," you say.

You collect your equipment from the jet and
head towards the weapons centre. Half a dozen
ALFs are attacking the building. Area 51 forces

are fighting back as best they can.

You take out your BAM and prepare yourself for the fight.

To try and pick off the aliens one at a time, go to 2.

To try and destroy them all in one shot, go to 49.

23

You continue to shoot at the enemy. One final blast with your ZAP finishes them off.

As you move carefully past the lifeless bodies, your MAAD flashes red — one of the ALFs is still alive!

To question it, go to 36.

To use your BAM on it, go to 14.

24

You call up Cranberry and explain the situation.

"So we have to close the portal at their end," he says.

"Exactly! But that needs someone to travel through the wormhole, close it up at their end; but before it closes up, somehow get back here.

Oh, yes, and rescue the kidnapped ALFs."

"Nothing too easy then," replies Cranberry.
"It could be done. If you set a timing device on a
bomb, you could rescue the ALFs and get through
the wormhole before it detonates and destroys
the alien portal."

"How long would the timing device need to be
set for?" you ask.

"Interesting question. I don't know the
answer."

To close the Area 51 portal, go to 21.

**To head through the wormhole and destroy
the alien portal, go to 27.**

25

You clean off Cranberry's gunge and head to the
Ops room in the heart of Arcane Manor.

But before you can assess your latest training
session, the 3D comms console bursts into life.
A holographic image of the Director General of
G.H.O.S.T. appears.

"Good afternoon, Agent. We have a Priority
One case for you. I am sending over details of
this mission via the encryption channel.

Good luck. You're going to need it."

To continue with the training debrief, go to 38.

To look at the mission immediately, go to 4.

26

Before the ALFs can react, you blast them with the BAM. You wonder how they knew you were coming. Someone back at Area 51 must have told them! *This makes things even harder*, you think.

To look for the captured ALFs, go to 18.
To set the gamma ray bomb and head back to Earth, go to 39.

27

"We have to try and rescue the kidnapped ALFs and close the wormhole up on the alien side, no matter what the risk is," you tell the doctor and general. "Take me to your wormhole portal."

You are taken through steel lined corridors to the huge vault containing the entrance to the wormhole.

"Impressive," you say. "So what sort of weapon will close up the portal on the alien side?"

"A gamma bomb," replies the general. "It's small enough to carry but powerful enough to do the job."

"Can you fit a timing device to it?" you ask.

The general nods. "Yes, I'll have our people sort that out. It should be ready in an hour."

Go to 33.

28

"We'll head to the command centre and get more information," you say.

You arrive to find General Walker waiting for you.

"Why are you here and not at the weapons centre, Agent?" he snaps. "I thought you were going to take on the ALFs?"

Before you can reply, a trooper rushes in.

"Enemy forces have taken over the weapons centre. They have the total-destruction lasers!"

"Then we're finished!" roars the general. "Abandon the base!"

Before you can react, there is a huge explosion that destroys the command centre and all within it. And that includes you!

You should have attacked the ALFs, not talked about them! Go back to 1.

29

You know that you are doomed, but you can still make sure the portal closes. You press the gamma ray detonator.

There is a flash of light as the chamber and the portal disintegrate.

You've saved the world but at the ultimate cost. Go back to 1.

30

You tell the general and doctor about the captain.

"Are there any more hostile aliens on the base?" you ask.

The doctor shrugs. "The ALFs attacking the weapons centre were the only ones we know about. But if they managed to take control of the captain, then perhaps they have passed on some kind of alien virus. Anyone could have been contaminated."

The general stares at you. "Even you, Agent."

"And you too, General," you reply.

If you've already heard about Project Wormhole, go to 12.

If you haven't, go to 46.

You set the timer and step through the portal.
Once again you feel as though you are being
ripped apart. Then there is flash of light and a
roaring noise. You realise the bomb has exploded.

The wormhole begins to disintegrate around
you. *The delay wasn't long enough*, you think.
It's all over.

Suddenly there is a flash of lightning, and you
find yourself safely back in Area 51. General
Walker and Dr Dekka are waiting for you.

The portal implodes on itself, and the vault is
filled with showers of stars and bursts of
energy. Then there is silence. The wormhole
is no more.

You tell the general and Dr Dekka what happened.

"Well done, Agent," says the general.

"Thanks. There's just one thing bothering me," you say. "The ALF I spoke to said that its master was already here on Earth... So I got thinking, who didn't want me to destroy the portal? And why?"

To use your stun gun on the general, go to 11.

To use your MAAD, go to 50.

32

You blast at the monster on the right. It disappears in a blinding flash, but the monster on the left is still heading towards you at speed!

Before you can react, the creature hits you and bursts wide open, covering you in a green, evil-smelling slime.

Go to 47.

33

An hour later, you have the gamma bomb in your pack and you are ready to head into the wormhole.

The general straps the timing device onto your wrist.

"By how long will you delay the explosion?" he asks.

You shrug. "Cranberry still has no answer. And I won't be able to communicate with anyone once I go through the portal."

"Then you should take some troopers with you," suggests Dr Dekka.

"That puts my men at risk as well," growls the general.

To head into the wormhole on your own, go to 16.

To take the troopers with you, go to 3.

34

"Open fire," you shout, and then suddenly realise that you've made a BIG mistake.

The troops obey your order. Unfortunately, you are in their line of fire!

The captain goes down under a hail of bullets, but so do you!

That wasn't clever! Go back to 1.

35

"Evasive action!" you order the computer. It obeys and spins in a series of spirals and loops.

"INCOMING MISSILE!" screams the computer. You glance out of the window to see the alien still riding the missile and coming towards you. You can't shake it off!

To shoot at the missile, go to 13.

To activate the jet's defence shield, go to 6.

36

Using your TALK device you ask the alien where the captured ALFs are being held.

"Tell me," you say, "and I'll let you live."

"They are in a secure unit awaiting trial. But you will never find it!"

To deal with the ALF and look for the unit, go to 14.

To tell the ALF about the gamma ray bomb, go to 41.

37

You take out your gun and point it at the captain.

"Stop the car!"

The captain ignores you. "Death to humans, death to humans."

You have no option. You pull the trigger and the captain slumps forward. You grab the steering wheel and put on the handbrake. The SUV comes to a screeching halt just metres from the fuel tank.

That was close! You wonder how the captain came under the control of the ALFs and if there are any more personnel on the base that have been taken over. You decide to head to the command centre to tell General Walker what has happened.

Go to 7.

38

"Let's finish the debrief first," you say to Cranberry.

"Not a good idea, Agent," replies the butler. "The director said it was a Priority One case. The clue is in the name. PRIORITY!"

You realise that Cranberry is right. The director would not be contacting you if this wasn't critical.

Go to 4.

39

You take out the gamma ray bomb and place it by the portal. But before you can set the timing device, the chamber is suddenly filled with laser blasts and explosions. You spin round, weapon ready as another squad of ALF fighters storm in. You fire at them but there are too many to deal with.

Go to 29.

40

You try to open the door, but it is locked!

You lean across and grab hold of the

steering wheel, but the captain seems to have superhuman strength. He fights you off, flinging you against the car door.

"Death to humans, death to humans!"

You reach for your gun, but it is too late! The SUV smashes into the fuel tank and explodes.

Don't get into cars with strangers!
Go back to 1.

41

"I have a gamma ray bomb," you tell the ALF. "And it's powerful enough to blow this whole base up. Tell the guards to bring the prisoners to the portal. Or else..."

"You wouldn't use it," replies the ALF. "You would die as well."

"Try me," you say, taking out the bomb. "I just have to press this button..."

The ALF backs down. He speaks into his wrist communicator to the guards, relaying your instructions.

Go to 5.

Cranberry prepares and loads your weapons on board the Phantom Flyer, your specially equipped supersonic jet.

You are soon in the air, flying at incredible speed towards Area 51.

You radio back to Arcane Manor.

"Any further news?"

"I have been in touch with General Walker, the base commander," says Cranberry. "Hostile ALFs are trying to take over the base's weapons centre. Heaven knows what will happen if they manage to do it!"

You are approaching Area 51 when the jet's alarms sound. The computer's voice fills the cabin. "INCOMING MISSILE!"

You look out of the cabin and are amazed to see an ALF riding on top of a missile, coming straight for you! *How is it doing that?* you wonder!

To shoot at the missile, go to 13.

To take evasive action, go to 35.

To activate the jet's defence shield, go to 6.

"Don't shoot! You'll hit me!" you shout.

The captain tightens his grip around your throat. You lash out with your foot and catch him. He staggers back and you attack using your jujutsu fighting skills.

You hold him in a headlock. "Tell me who you are," you say.

"My master will win," he rasps. "Death to humans!"

You realise that somehow the captain has been taken over by the ALFs. Before you can ask him any more questions, he breaks free. One of the troops fires at the captain, taking him down.

You stand over the captain's lifeless body.

"That's a shame. We could have got some useful information from him."

You decide to head to the command centre to tell General Walker what has happened.

Go to 7.

44

When you come to, you find yourself strapped to a metal table. Several ALFs are standing over you. One is holding some sort of laser drill.

He points it at you and switches it on.

The last sounds you hear are your own screams.

Ouch! That hurt. Go back to 1.

45

You land the jet and taxi towards the main reception area.

You are greeted by a troop of soldiers and you introduce yourself to the captain.

"Glad you're here, Agent. We could do with some help. The ALFs are still laying siege to the weapons centre," he tells you. "General Walker is in the command centre. Where do you want to go?"

To go to the weapons centre, go to 22.
To head to the command centre, go to 28.

46

"Tell me about the project," you say.

"We have been working with various friendly ALFs over the past few years," replies Dr Dekka.

"They crash-landed on Earth," explains the general. "They were grateful to us for our kind treatment of them, so they agreed to help us develop our technology."

Dr Dekka continues. "One of the projects was to develop a way of visiting other planets, millions of light years away. This is impossible in spacecraft, but it could be done by using wormholes."

She clicks a button and a 3D model of a wormhole appears.

"And you can use them to travel through time and space, as proposed by Albert Einstein in his theory of general relativity."

"I thought wormholes were just a theory," you say.

Dr Dekka smiles. "Not any more, we have one here on Area 51."

If you've already heard about the ALF situation on the base, go to 12.

If you haven't, go to 30.

The cellar lights flash on. You shield your eyes against the sudden glare as a voice booms out from loudspeakers. It is Cranberry, your butler and fellow G.H.O.S.T. agent.

"Oh dear, Agent. You should have used the MAAD. That would have shown you which monster was real and which one was merely a virtual reality reflection."

"Sorry, Cranberry. I'll remember to tell the MAAD to detect the monster next time." You wipe the slime from your hair. "How do you make this stuff?"

"My special top secret recipe. It's been passed down the ages from Cranberry to Cranberry. Now it's time for a debrief..."

Go to 25.

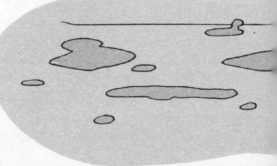

48

You head towards a door in the wall of the corridor. It is locked, but a blast with your weapon soon opens it. However, the ALFs know where you are. The air fills with streams of laser bolts and blast grenades as you dive through the doorway. You look around — there is no way out!

A grenade pops through the doorway and lands on the floor. There is a flash of light and afterwards, nothing...

You got yourself trapped! Go back to 1.

49

You set the BAM to maximum power, aim at the centre of the group of ALFs and pull the trigger. A bolt of energy shoots from the BAM and instantly vaporises the attackers.

"Secure this centre," you tell the captain. "I need to talk to General Walker."

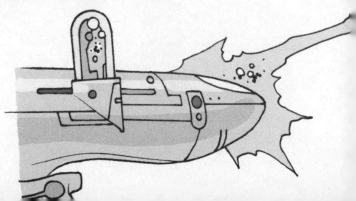

The captain stares at you.

"Are you sure that's a good idea?" he says.

"Why wouldn't it be?" you ask.

"Er… no reason," he replies. "I'll take you to him."

You are puzzled by the captain's manner.

To get the captain to take you to the general, go to 10.

To question the captain further, go to 17.

"Let's see who the bad apple is. Detect!"
You switch on the MAAD. It flashes a red laser
beam, targeting Dr Dekka.

"So, you found me!" she bellows. "Too bad
you're too late!" Her outer skin splits in half,
revealing a slavering ALF. Her tongue shoots out
towards you, but you dodge it and fire.

The creature explodes in an instant, covering you with green slime. *Not again*, you think...

The general looks dumbfounded.

"I can't believe Dr Dekka was an alien. How?"

"I'm afraid we'll probably never know the answer," you reply.

"Did you ever think the ALF was me?" asks the general.

"Not really," you say. "I wanted to put her, or rather, it, off guard for a moment."

Your comms link flashes. It is Cranberry.

"I think that a two-minute delay would be a good time to set, Agent."

"Slow, but appreciated." You laugh and tell him about the mission. "And get the hot water on," you finish. "I need to get rid of some slime."

"It's the least I can do," he replies. "Well done, Agent. You've saved the planet. You're a real hero!"

G.H.O.S.T.

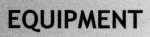

EQUIPMENT

Phantom Flyer: For fast international and intercontinental travel, you use the Phantom Flyer, a supersonic business jet crammed full of detection and communication equipment and weaponry.

Spook Trucks: For more local travel you use one of G.H.O.S.T.'s fleet of Spook Trucks — heavily armed and armoured SUVs you requisition from local agents.

MAAD (Monster and Alien Detector)

BAM (Blasts All Monsters)

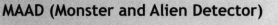

ZAP gun (Zero Alien Presence when used)

TALK (Translates all living knowledge)

MONSTER HUNTER

I HERO

ZOMBIE

STEVE BARLOW ◇ STEVE SKIDMORE

Illustrated by PAUL DAVIDSON

EDGE

You are an agent of **G.H.O.S.T.** — Global Headquarters Opposing Supernatural Threats.

Our world is under constant attack from supernatural horrors that lurk in the shadows. It's your job to make sure they stay there.

You are in the dining room. Your butler comes towards you carrying a covered silver dish. The dish is making bleeping noises.

"Your phone, Agent."

"Thank you, Cranberry." You check the screen. You have an email from the Director General of G.H.O.S.T.

"I think she wants me to get a move on," you say.

To set off immediately for Beijing, go to 37.

To research zombies first, go to 25.

Continue the adventure in:

MONSTER HUNTER

ZOMBIE

About the 2Steves

"The 2Steves" are
Britain's most popular
writing double act
for young people,
specialising in comedy
and adventure. They
perform regularly in schools and libraries,
and at festivals, taking the power of words
and story to audiences of all ages.

Together they have written many books,
including the *I HERO Immortals* and *iHorror* series.

About the illustrator:
Paul Davidson

Paul Davidson is a British
illustrator and comic book artist.

I HERO Legends — collect them all!

ATHENA

978 1 4451 5234 9 pb
978 1 4451 5235 6 ebook

BEOWULF

978 1 4451 5225 7 pb
978 1 4451 5226 4 ebook

KING ARTHUR

978 1 4451 5231 8 pb
978 1 4451 5232 5 ebook

FREYA

978 1 4451 5237 0 pb
978 1 4451 5238 7 ebook

HERCULES

978 1 4451 5228 8 pb
978 1 4451 5229 5 ebook

ROBIN HOOD

978 1 4451 5183 0 pb
978 1 4451 5184 7 ebook

Have you read the I HERO Atlantis Quest mini series?

MENACE FROM THE DEEP
Steve Barlow - Steve Skidmore
978 1 4451 2867 2 pb
978 1 4451 2868 9 ebook

OCEAN ALLIANCE
Steve Barlow - Steve Skidmore
978 1 4451 2870 2 pb
978 1 4451 2871 9 ebook

BATTLE FOR THE SEAS
Steve Barlow - Steve Skidmore
978 1 4451 2876 4 pb
978 1 4451 2877 1 ebook

ATLANTIS ASSAULT
Steve Barlow - Steve Skidmore
978 1 4451 2873 3 pb
978 1 4451 2874 0 ebook

Also by the 2Steves...

978 1 4451 5104 5 pb
978 1 4451 5119 9 eBook

You are a skilled, stealthy ninja. Your village has been attacked by a warlord called Raiden. Now YOU must go to his castle and stop him before he destroys more lives.

978 1 4451 5101 4 pb
978 1 4451 5117 5 eBook

You are the Warrior Princess. Someone wants to steal the magical ice diamonds from the Crystal Caverns. YOU must discover who it is and save your kingdom.

978 1 4451 5103 8 pb
978 1 4451 5121 2 eBook

You are a magical unicorn. Empress Yin Yang has stolen Carmine, the red unicorn. Yin Yang wants to destroy the colourful Rainbow Land. YOU must stop her!

978 1 4451 5102 1 pb
978 1 4451 5124 3 eBook

You are a spy, codenamed Scorpio. Someone has taken control of secret satellite laser weapons. YOU must find out who is responsible and stop their dastardly plans.